MW00633496

Book One

Dedicated to Daisy, a master of words, art, and music.
Special thanks to Samantha Delman-Caserta, Raymond Rodriquez,
and Donna Schofield.

Charlotte's New York Adventure
Copyright © 2019 by Dunton Publishing

(Book 1) *A Girl with a Mission (June 2016)*
(Book 2) *A Meeting in Midtown (February 2018)*
(Book 3) *A Girl Takes the Lead (October 2018)*

Lese is a writer from the upper west side of Manhattan.

Ena is an illustrator from the Olympic city of Sarajevo. (enahodzic.com)

ISBN: 978-0692732809

duntonpublishing.com

Charlotte's
New York Adventure

A girl with a mission

Lese Dunton

Lese Dunton

illustrations by Ena Hodzic

Charlotte was in a bad mood.

Fortunately, her father understood
that walking around New York City
can be good for you.

So he drove her over the river
and through the neighborhoods.

Then they walked and they walked
and they talked and they talked.

By the end of the day,
he asked her two very interesting questions.

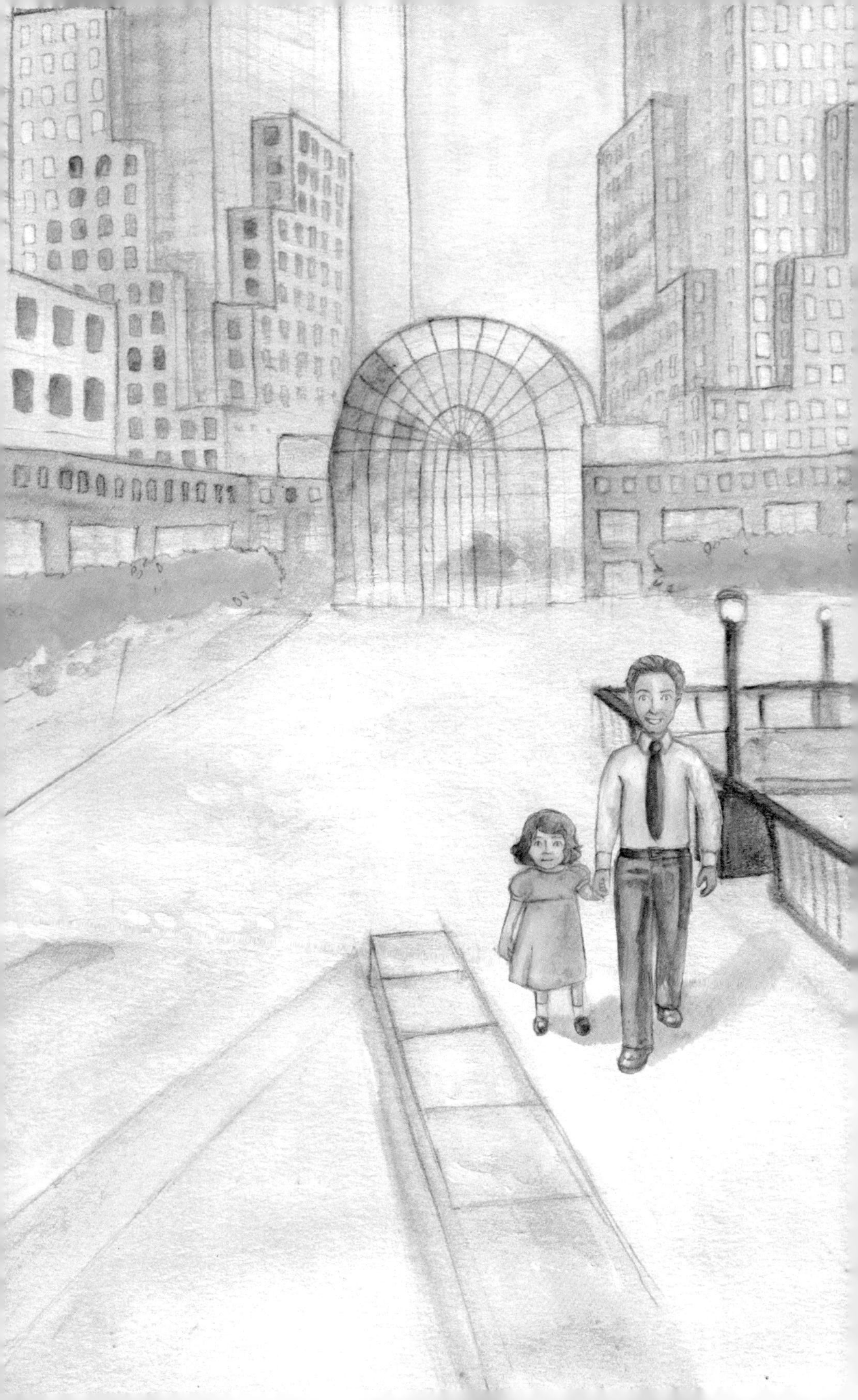

Do you like New York City?

Yes - replied Charlotte.

Do you want to live here when you grow up?

I think so...

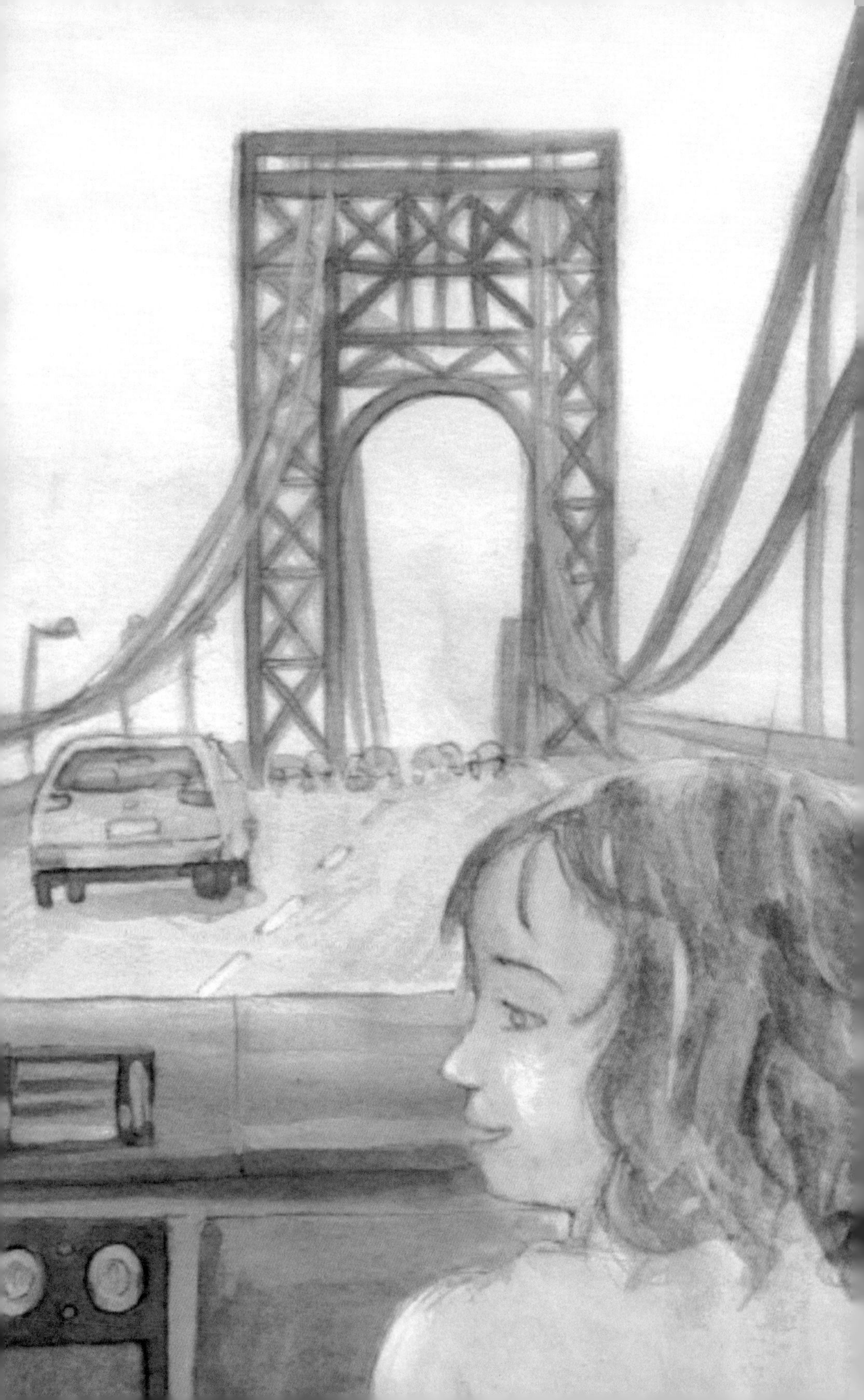

I do love this big ol' bridge.

It reaches pretty high - to a blue and open sky.

I could take magical flights and see sparkling sights.

Why should I doubt? I'll just give a glad shout.

There must be a way we can make this all work out...

It's not always that easy, Charlotte my dear.
It could take work, and what about fear?

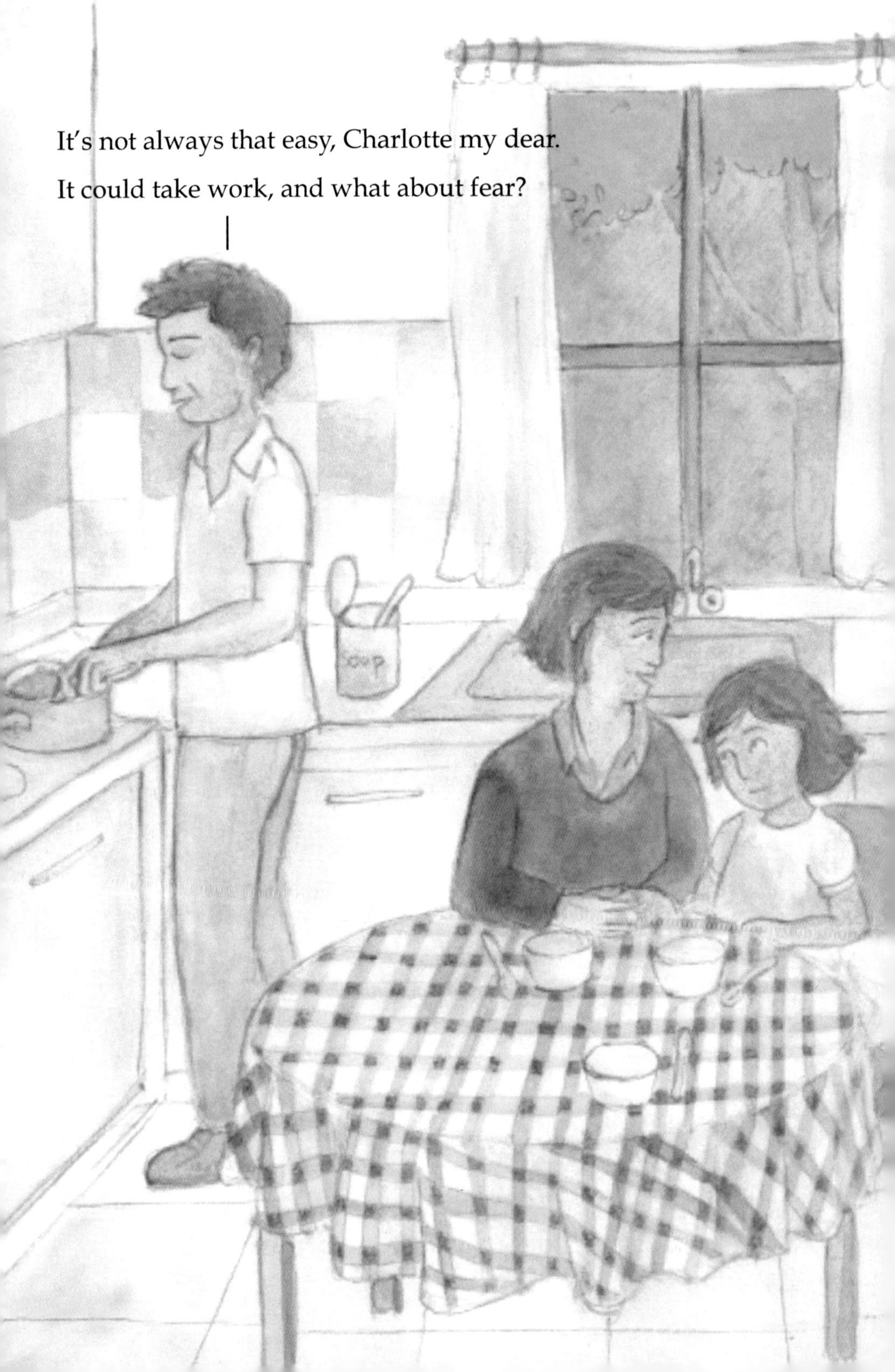
Soup

Hey Mom, guess what?
I'm making a plan -
to live in the city.
I'm pretty sure I can.

— No worries, my angel, I know you are brave.
Like that time at Jones Beach when you faced a big wave.
You're good at solving problems,
I see you have a flair.
Plus you listen to your friends
when they need someone to care...

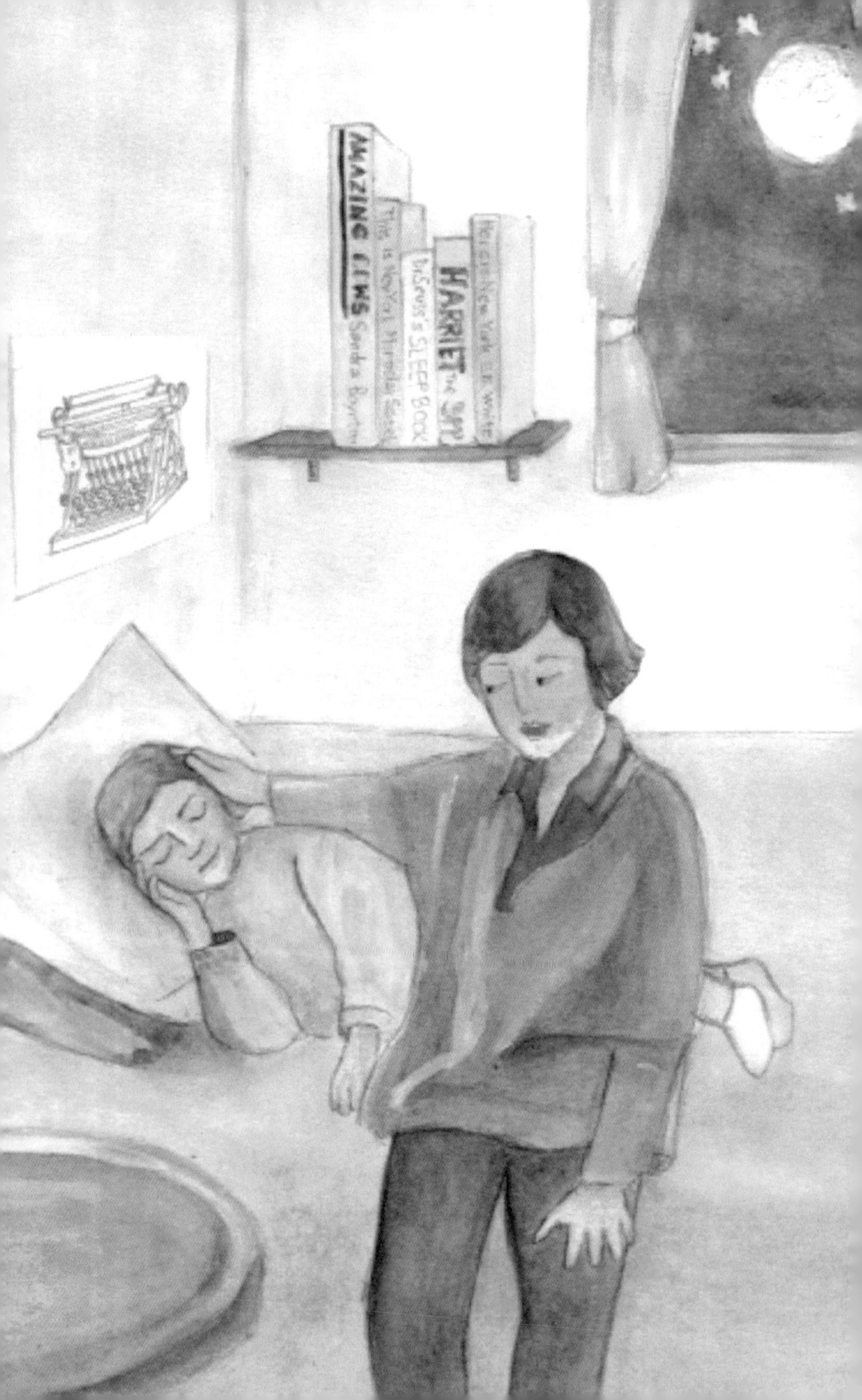
AMAZING
HARRIET
SLEEP BOOK

...There's nothing you can't do that you set your mind to, and there's no one else who's smarter - or more fabulous - than you!

(Mom breaks into song):

♪♫ I want to see for myself
Those faraway places
I've been reading about
in a book that I took from a shelf.

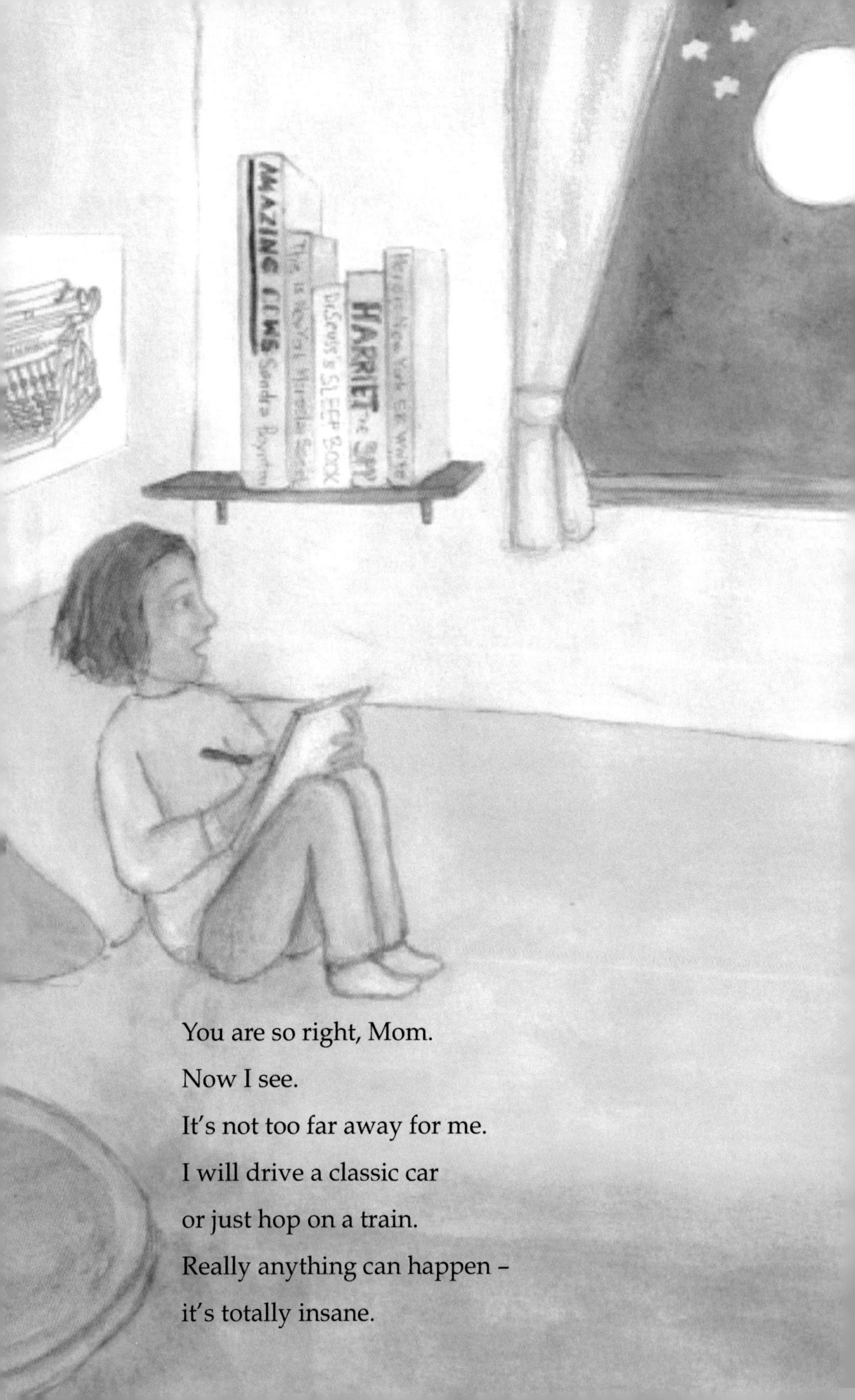
HARRIET
SLEEP BOOK

You are so right, Mom.

Now I see.

It's not too far away for me.

I will drive a classic car

or just hop on a train.

Really anything can happen –

it's totally insane.

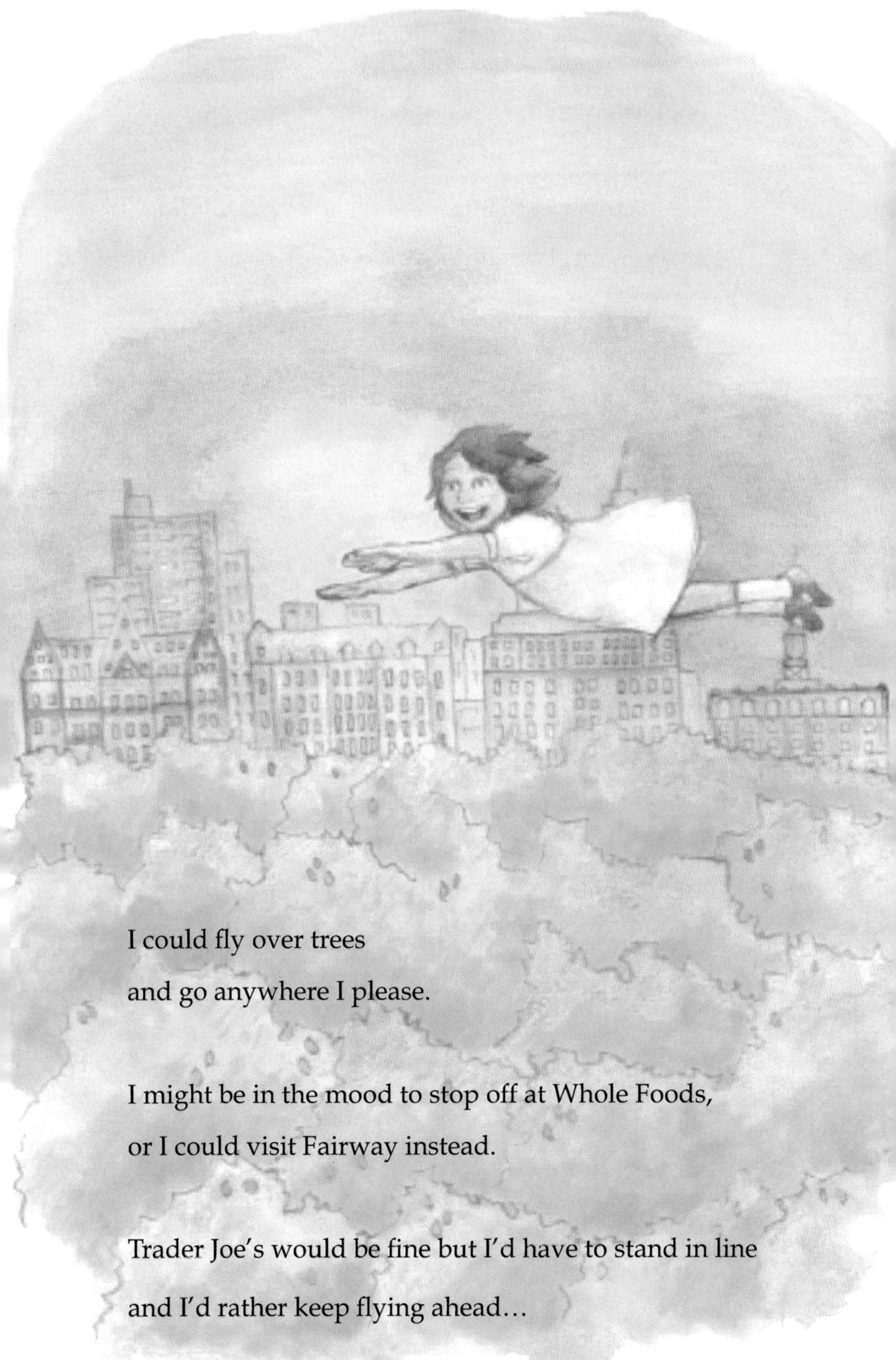

I could fly over trees
and go anywhere I please.

I might be in the mood to stop off at Whole Foods,
or I could visit Fairway instead.

Trader Joe's would be fine but I'd have to stand in line
and I'd rather keep flying ahead…

I’ll compose at the piano and dream a brilliant song,
Fans can listen on their headphones, all day long.

My friend Adele, she sings so well, all about love and loss.
Deep within me, I find music - like it’s from a cosmic boss.

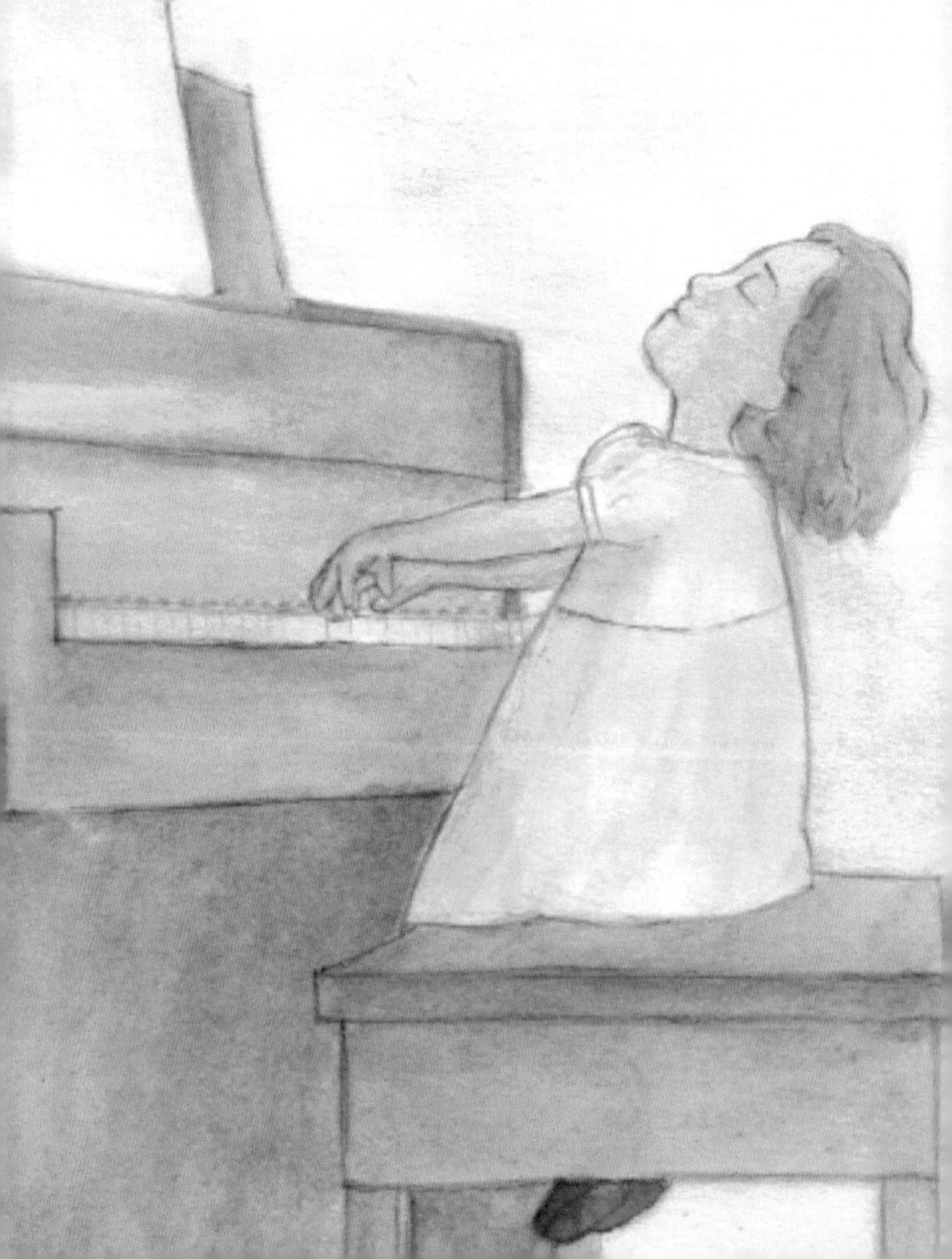

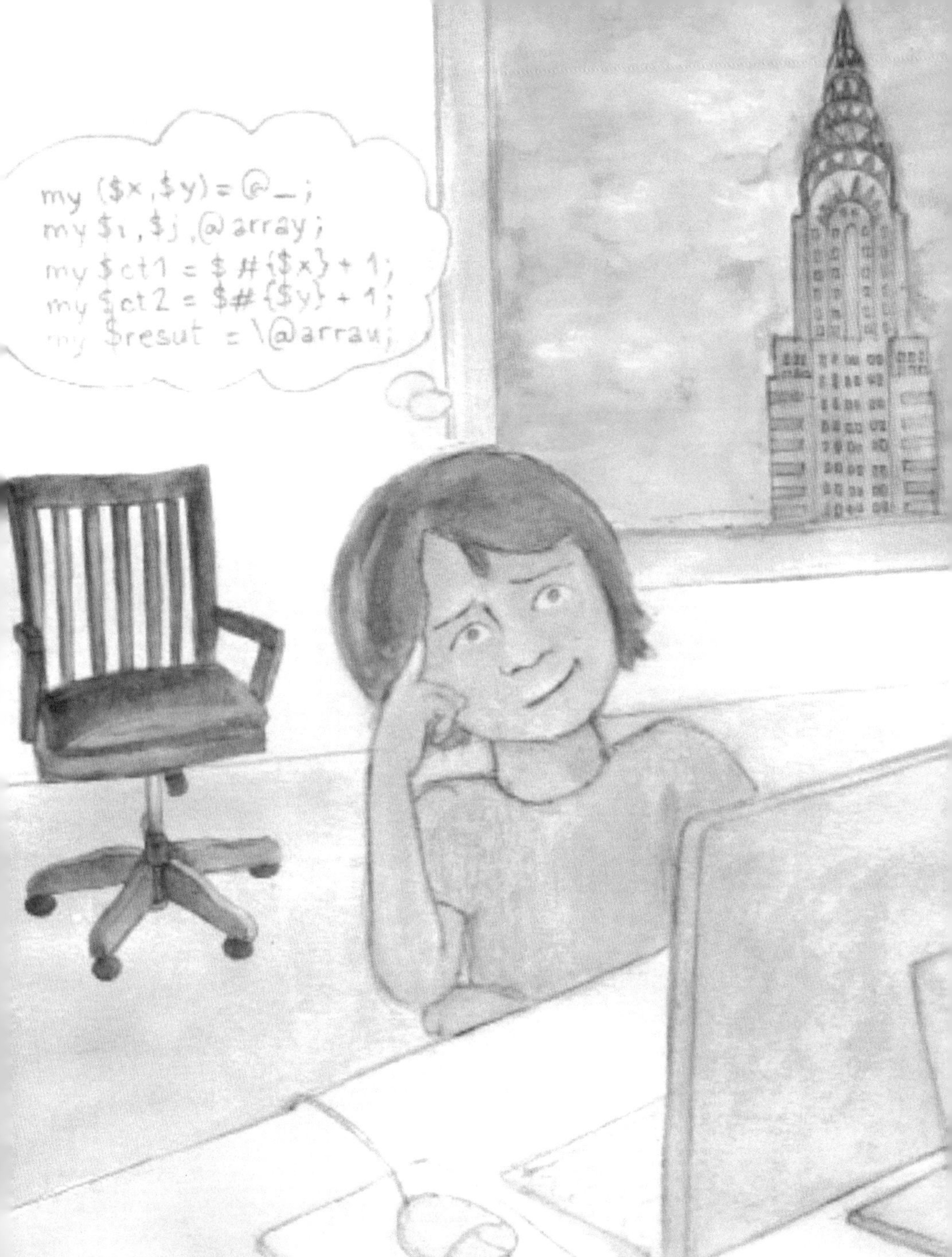
my ($x,$y)=@_;
my $i,$j,@array;
my $ct1 = $#{$x} + 1;
my $ct2 = $#{$y} + 1;
my $resut = \@array;

On the computer, I program helpful stuff.

Handy solutions when times are tough.

Writing great code is like writing a letter.

This app makes your bad health get better and better.

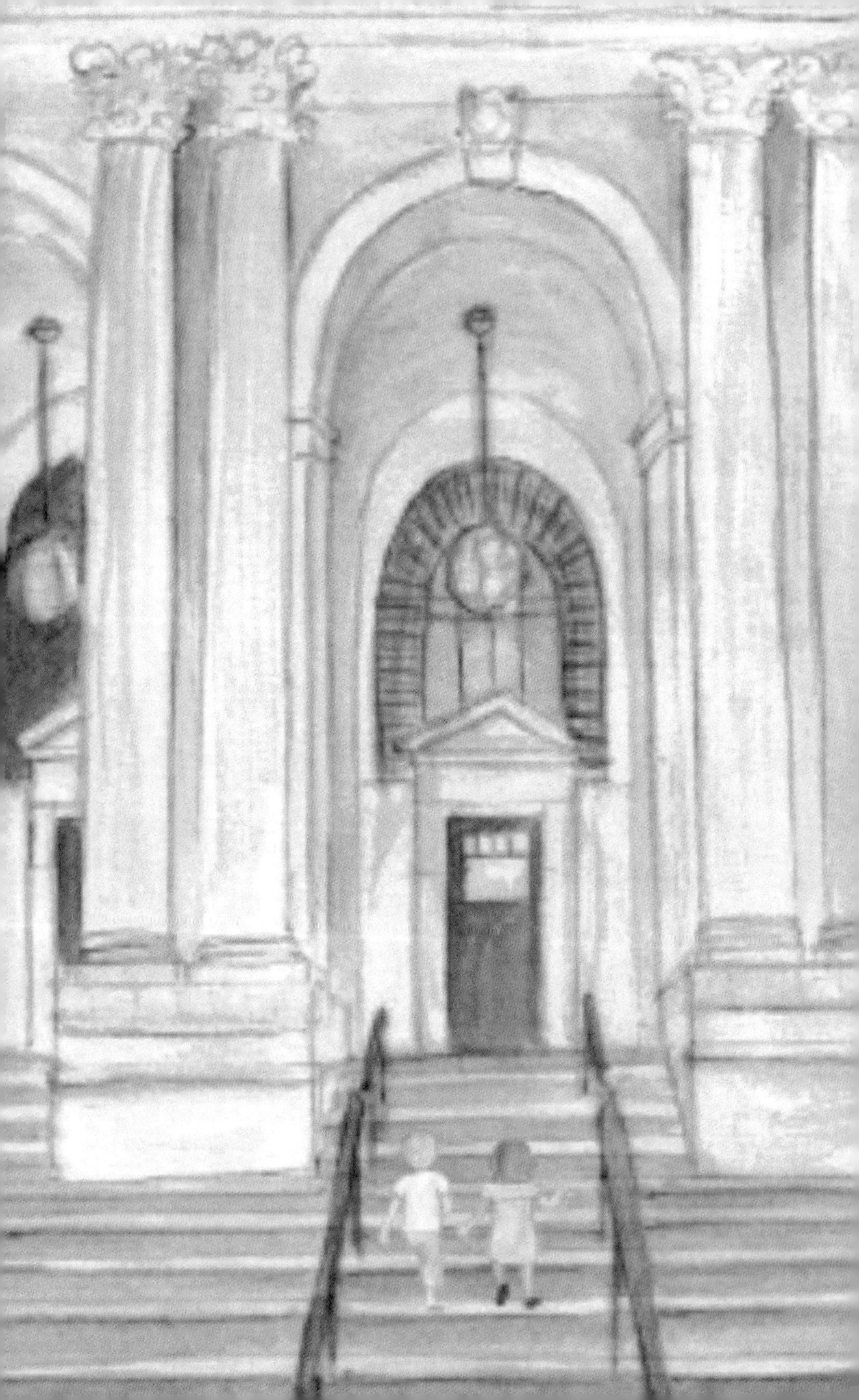

That boy Keith wants to hear every detail of her life.

I flew at my best,

right on Central Park West.

Then I wrote a cool song, so people sing along...

I developed an app that loads up quick...

it cures patients when they're sick...

and then I...

Keith: Wow. I'm impressed!

The next day at school, it's back to reality...

You've been acting so cheerful, it seems kind of strange.

Did something within you just happen to change?

I'm drafting a plan, and it's totally fun,
like the warm morning sun or a game that you've won.
I'm so much in awe of all that I draw,
and I'm happy to find that it starts in the mind.

Don't you think that it might be both scary and yucky?

No, I think that I'll be both courageous and lucky.

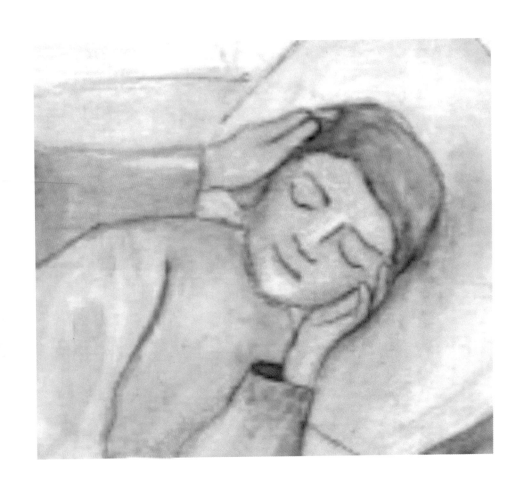

At bedtime,

after Mom sings the nice song again,

Charlotte floats into a cozy sleep and starts to dream...

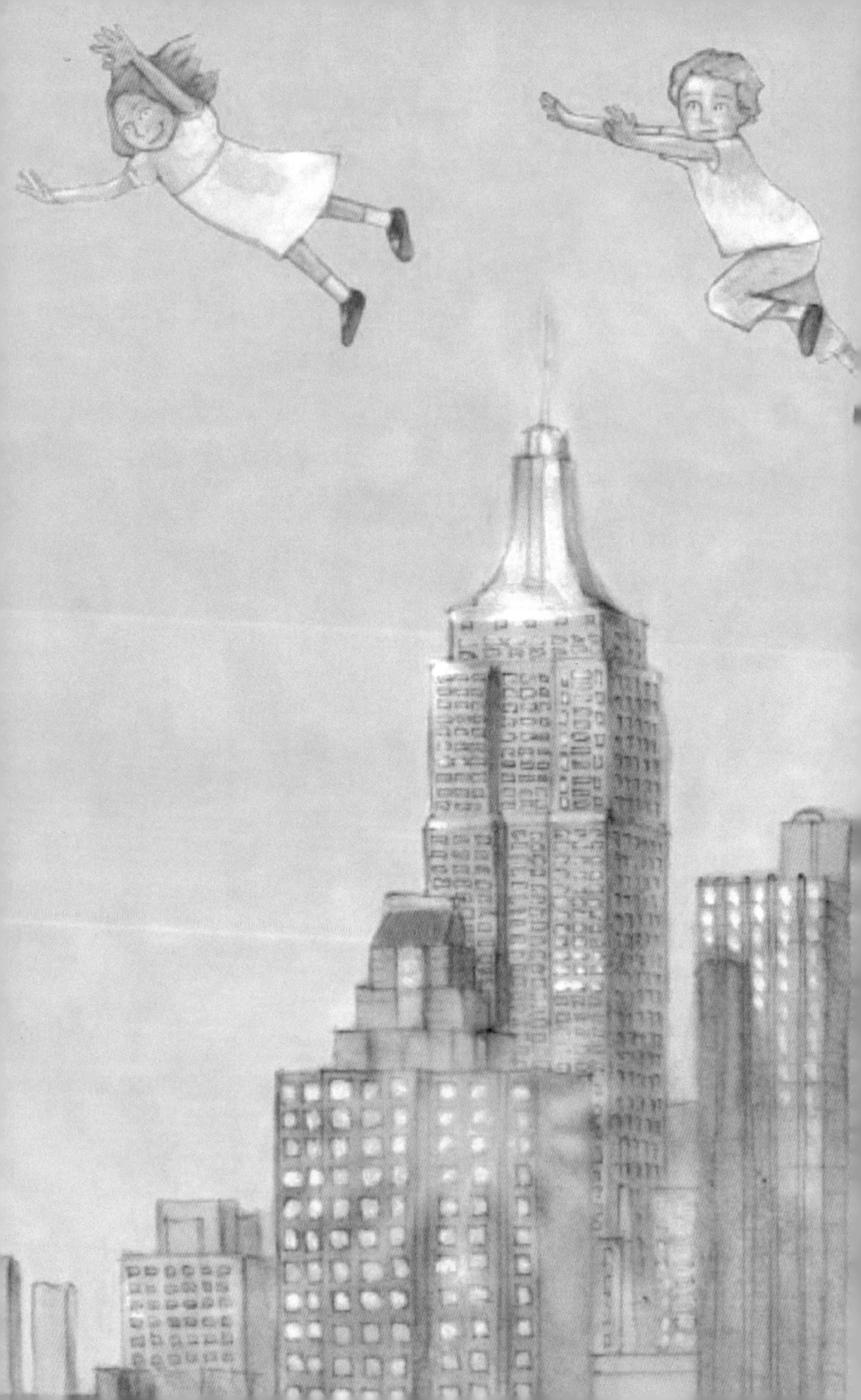

They call this building the Empire State.

Just try flying over it, you'll feel great!

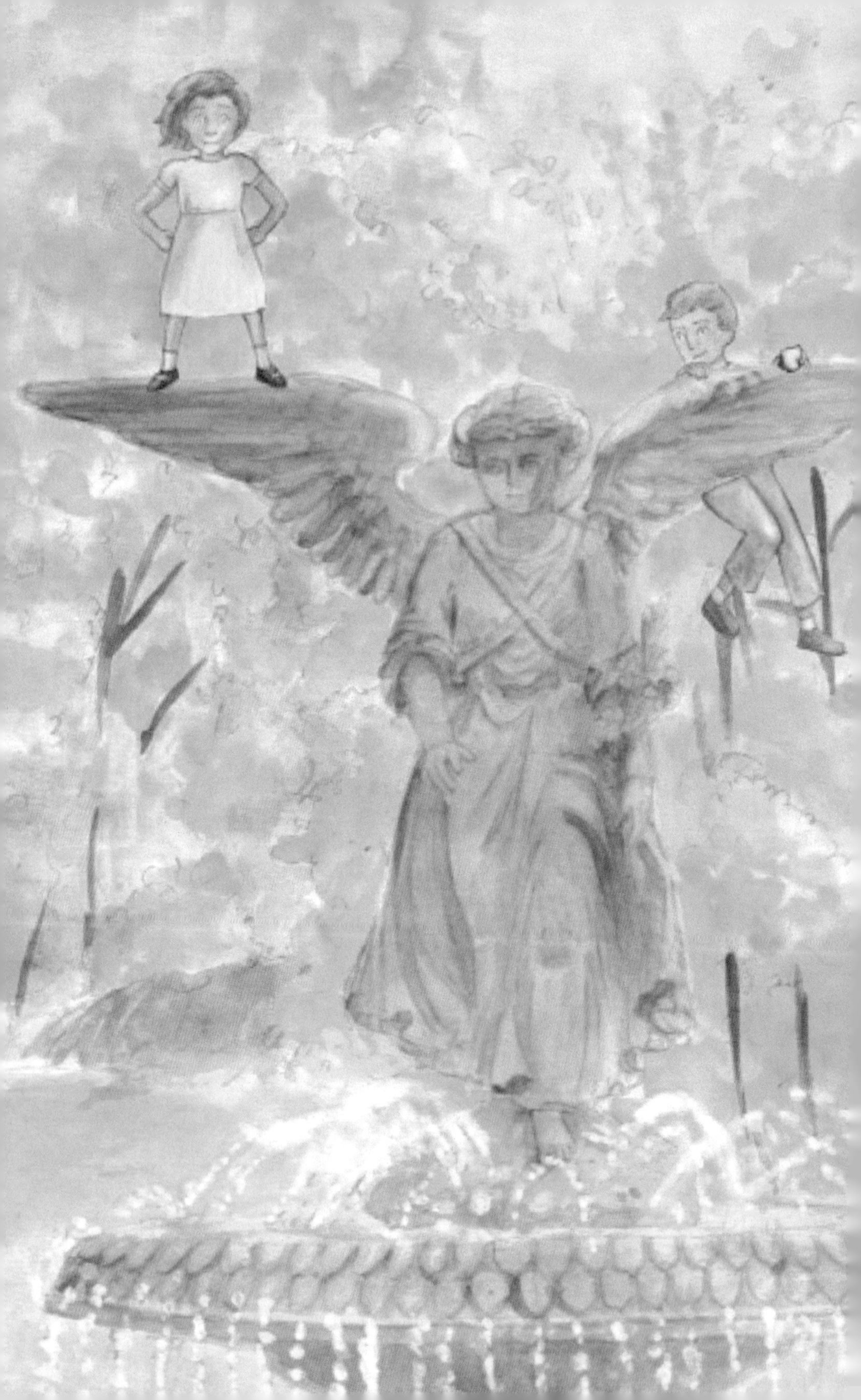

When you reach Bethesda Fountain,
it's like standing on a mountain.

Her wings give strength and powers
while you breathe in healing flowers.

Surrounded by trees, you will feel a nice breeze,
and start flying again with great ease.

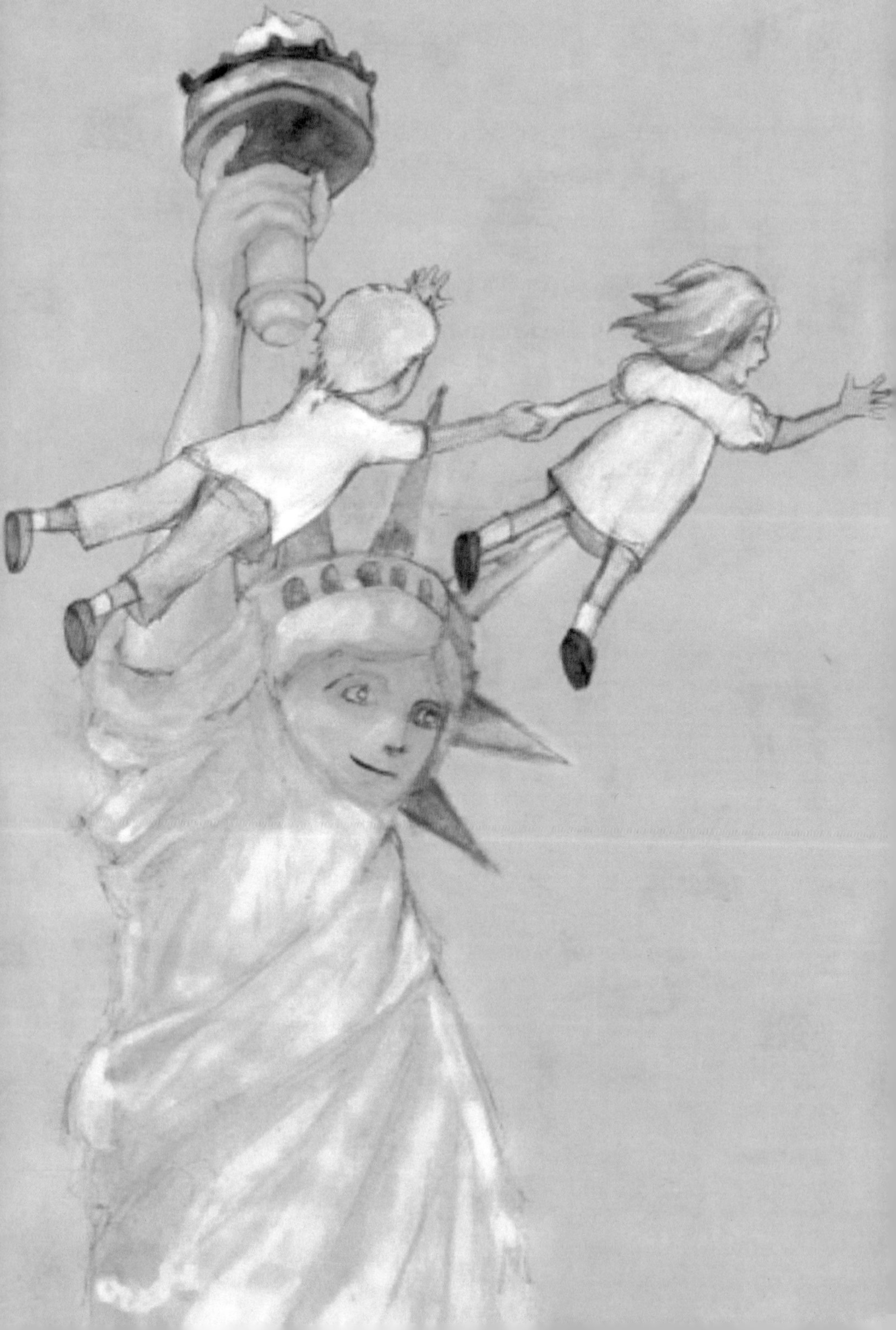

Statue of Liberty:

I see you're a leader, for goodness' sakes.

That's excellent, Charlotte, you've got what it takes.

Such the New Yorker now, through and through.

Come on in, I lift my big lamp up for you.

Charlotte:

Oh Green Copper Lady, it must be fate.

I have a secret mission – we should collaborate.

We can use our special talents to enlighten the land.

I think you can imagine it and understand.

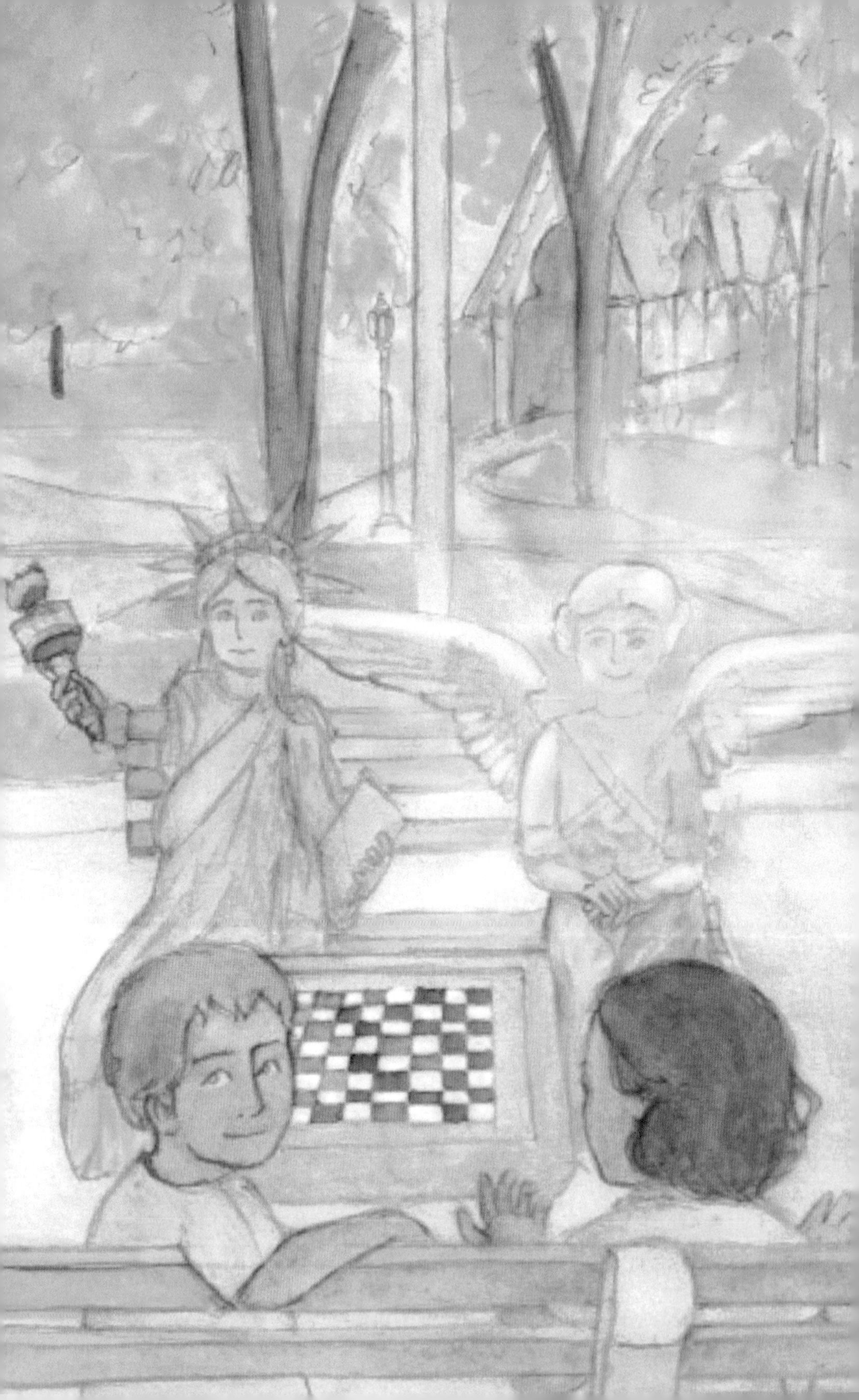

Angel Beth from the Fountain can glow in the dark,
so we'll have important meetings in Central Park.

When we put our heads together we can fight despair
and help people of the world feel as light as air.

We make such a cool team, given all that we know.
So Beth and Green Lady - *you ready to go?*

"Ready when you are," they say in one voice.
"And hey thanks for asking, you've made a good choice."

Where to begin and what will it be?
They'll take the next step and then we shall see...

Charlotte can lead them and figure it out,
now that she's let go of fear and self-doubt.

And so they'll allow all their dreams to uncork,
a girl with her team and a plan....in New York!

To be continued.

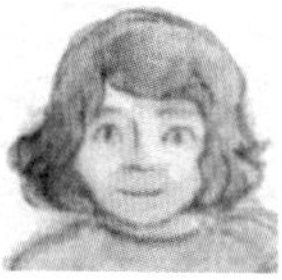

Would you like to get on Charlotte's invitation list? You'll receive a free ebook illustrated by legendary Raggedy Ann and Andy creator Johhny Gruelle.

Email: charlottemissionclues@gmail.com.

Made in the USA
Middletown, DE
11 January 2022